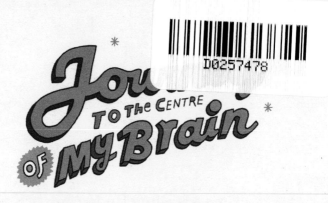

Ever met an alien? **JAMES CARTER** is probably the closest you'll ever get. A prize-winning poet, wild guitarist and professional dreamer, he's written loads of poetry books and even stuff for the telly. He zooms all over the cosmos (well, the UK and abroad) in his UFO (well, trains, actually) to meet and greet aliens (well, visit schools and libraries and festivals) and do very lively poetry performances and workshops (yes, that bit's true).

When on planet earth, James lives in Oxfordshire with his earthling family – his one wife, two daughters, three cats and four guitars, all of which are called Keith (that's the guitars, by the way). Good luck on your journey into James's brain . . .

Raised by wild guinea pigs in the jungles of West Yorkshire, **CHRIS GARBUTT** developed the uncanny ability to emit funny pictures with his mind. He now works out of a giant blue airship hovering two miles above central London and only ever comes to the earth's surface to buy cakes.

Also by James Carter

Time-travelling Underpants

With Brian Moses

Greetings, Earthlings!

With Graham Denton

Wild! Rhymes That Roar

Journey TO THE CENTRE OF MY Brain

POEMS BY JAMES CARTER

Illustrated by Chris Garbutt

MACMILLAN CHILDREN'S BOOKS

First published 2012 by Macmillan Children's Books
a division of Macmillan Publishers Limited
20 New Wharf Road, London N1 9RR
Basingstoke and Oxford
Associated companies throughout the world
www.panmacmillan.com

ISBN 978-0-230-75195-8

Text copyright © James Carter 2012
Ilustrations copyright © Chris Garbutt 2012

1 3 5 7 9 8 6 4 2

A CIP catalogue record for this book is available from
the British Library.

Printed and bound by CPI Group (UK) Ltd, Croydon CR0 4YY

ACKNOWLEDGEMENTS

As ever and for ever, for the three that make this journey with me – Sarah, Lauren and Madeleine (Moley) – with all my love. And so you know – 'You, by Me' is for Sarah, 'Life of Flight' is for Lauren, 'What Did You Do at School Today?' is for Madeleine (Moley), 'The Cat' is for uber-tabby Alice and 'This Is Where . . .' is for the very wonderful South Moreton Primary School. Oh yes, and thanks too to Jules Verne for letting me 'borrow' his title.

With a big bunch of thanks to some real top bananas: Gaby Morgan for her endless encouragement; Graham Denton for being such a brilliant poetry chum, and all those fantastic classes and teachers in all those super schools for making me feel so very welcome!

www.jamescarterpoet.co.uk

CONTENTS

!!!!!!!
Last night I had
the strangest DREAM.
I'm in a CAVERN dark and deep.
The like before I've NEVER seen . . .
I try, but fail to wake from SLEEP.
COBWEBS cluster on the walls. Echoes
ECHO to and fro. MOSS is forming on
the floors. SQUEALS and scuttles
come and go. And so, I journeyed
. . . through MY BRAIN.
I won't be going
there
!!!
!!!
!!!
!!!!!!!! A G A I N !!!!!!!!
!!!
!!!!
!!   !!
!!   !!
!!   !!
!!!!!!   !!!!!!

1

I'm the BOSS of the Universe

I'm at my mate Robert Baker's
for a sleepover in his tent.

*

It's freezing cold, it's really late
and we can't get to sleep
and we're feeling a bit icky
having had half a packet
of chocolate biscuits each.

So we tell each other jokes.
We do animal shapes in the torchlight.
We tell each other really scary stories.
And still we can't sleep, so Robert says,
'Hey, let's play I'm the Boss of the Universe!'
'What's that?' I say. 'Well . . .' he says,
'you just say what you'd do if you were Boss of
    the Universe.'

*

So I say, 'OK. You start.'

So he says: 'Children are allowed to drive cars!'

So I say: 'OK, children are allowed to drive cars,
    and tractors, helicopters and submarines!'

So he says: 'Children have three birthdays a year!'

So I say: 'OK, children have three birthdays a
    year . . . and are granted three wishes *every
    week*!'

So he says: 'Children have to go on space
    missions!'

So I say: 'OK, children have to go on space
    missions to other planets and meet and greet
    ALIENS!'

And we laugh and we laugh and we can't stop
    laughing.
But then the torch goes off. And it goes quiet.
    Very quiet.
And it goes dark. Really really dark.
    And somewhere a door bangs.
And we're all trembly and quivery in our sleeping
    bags.
Then there's a shadow, and a ghostly voice
    whispers through the darkness . . .

'Would the Boss of the Universe go to sleep if he
    had his favourite *teddy bear*?'

The ReallyReallyReally TrulyTrueTruth About . . . Teddy Bears

Everybody has a teddy.
Even if they say they don't, they do,
they're fibbing. Even kings, queens,

famous footballers, hairy rock stars
and busy teachers. Yours included.
And all those people on the telly. Them too.

And I'm sure even aliens have their own
equally cute, equally cuddly, equally
dog-eared, squished and dribbled-over

version of this classic soft toy. But why?
Well, why not? However old you are,
however grown up you may appear to be,

however important or bossy you become,
in a hush of a moment every now and then,
you will still feel the need to open

the bedroom cupboard, remove
that little fuzzy bundle, and give it
a sniff and a kiss and a little snuggle.

Fancy Talk

Hey look!

Where?

Over there!
It's a brilliant blend
of rain and sun
of liquid and light
all superbly celebrated
in a celestial spectrum
of seven heavenly hues,
all colour-coded in
precipitating particles.

Oh . . . you mean a RAINBOW?

Err . . . yeah!

A MARVEL
of a **MARBLE**
MORE STABLE
than a
ST★R
more
MAGICAL
than
moonshine
more
beautiful
by far.
Go **SEARCH**
this **BIG BLUE**
MARBLE
go see what
time has grown . . .
find **US**, find **LIFE**, find **LIVING**
it's *HERE*, it's *EARTH*
it's **HME**

What *Stars* Are

Stars
are not
the shards of glass
smashed by the gods in anger.

Neither
are they the sparkling souls
of intergalactic travellers.

They're not even
the blinking eyes
of invisible skywatchers.

No.

Stars
  are
    Stars.

The
dying embers
of ancient fires
that will never know how
they dazzle and delight
us with the final
flickers of their
lives.

The *Northern* Lights

are not
what
they seem.

Not fireworks
from another realm.

Not portals
into mystic dreams.

Not cosmic curtains, even
swarms of magic dust.

No. They're simply
solar particles
brought to us
on wild winds
bursting forth
in winter skies
like gifts
to soothe
our tired
eyes.

The *Moon* Speaks!

I, the moon,
would like it known – I
never follow people home. I
simply do not have the time. And
neither do I ever shine. For what you
often see at night is me reflecting solar
light. And I'm not cheese! No – none of
these: no mozzarellas, cheddars, bries, all
you'll find here – if you please – are my
dusty, empty seas. And cows do not
jump over me. Now that is simply
lunacy! You used to come and
visit me. Oh do return,
I'm lonely, see.

The *Wolf* Outside

I wake.   I know.
No need   to see.
A visitor has come for me. That
wolf is at the door again. In the
dark, the pouring rain. He makes
no sound – he needs to hear my
breath, my pulse, my thoughts,
my fear. We wait together. Two
souls still. I need to live, he
needs to kill. He leaves ... I
breathe. I sigh and how.
I check. The wolf
has gone,
for now.

The *Trespasser*

Whenever I go
down to the woods
at the weekends
Mum will give me
this warning.

You be careful. Don't go
near the air-raid shelter.
Don't jump into the bear pit.
Just stick to the path
and you beware of the fox.

There is no fox! I would say.
Until now. But this isn't the woods,
nothing so wild, just our
old back garden on a grey
January afternoon. I go
to kick the ball but stop,
for there beside me, by the hedge,
as big as a dog, all rusty red
and skulking about with its winter
coat and outsize tail, is a fox.
It steps so lightly, waits,
seems lost, like a wayward ghost
that has drifted too far
from the safety of night. Our eyes meet.

'Mum!' the word won't come out. 'Mum!'
I'm stiff with shock, too stunned to speak.
'Mum, it's a . . .' Nothing still. I turn to
the house, and know as soon as
I look again the trespasser
will have disappeared.
I turn around, then
back and see
I'm now all
alone.

Hungry Haiku

One moonwashed evening
a shadow with a brush tail
slips through the cornfields

Ever nearer now
whiskers are twitching for signs
of a late supper

Trembling in the dark
the feathered ones sense trouble:
will the farmer wake?

An Anti-ode-eo to La Mosquito

I'm covered in bites
and now I can't sleep-o.
I hope you feel bad
you nasty mosquito!

I wish you would cease-o
you pesky petite-o.
You've had quite a feast-o:
my neck, knees and feet-o!

Of all minibeast-o
I love you the least-o.
So beat a retreat-o.
It's time to FINITO . . .

Oh please-o, mosquito?

Do WOOLLY MAMMOTHS Have Nits?

Of course they do, you silly!
AND moths AND flies AND fleas,
AND cockroaches AND giant wasps
AND several swarms of bees.

Now cruise down to the chemist
and choose a giant jar
of Crush-the-Critters-Hit-the-Nits®
and then it's time to start –

to wash old Shnozzle with a hose
and shampoo him with care
and then apply a king-size comb
(though gently) through his hair.

You do this once or twice a day,
with plenty of rubs and scrubs,
for Fuzzy-Wuzzy must be rid
of nasty nitty bugs!

And when his coat's a flea-free zone
reward him with a treat:
a stinging-nettle sandwich or
a buttercup to eat!

LULLABY For a
WOOLLY MAMMOTH

(To the tune of 'Twinkle, Twinkle' . . .)

Woolly
mammoth,
hear me sing . . .
! go to sleep you hairy thing!
! You   can snooze outside my
! door   . . . just as long as you don't
!   !   snore. Come on, Shaggy, shut
!   your eyes,   now it's
time for   beddy-byes!

WHat Are DiNOS Made oF?

Grr! Grr! Grr!
Grr!Grr!Grr!
Grr!
Grr!Grr!
Grr!
Grr!
Grr!
Grr!
Grr!
Grr!   Grr!   Grr!
Grr!Grr!Grr!Grr!
Grr!   Grr!   Grr!
Grr!Grr!
Grr!Grr!Grr!
Grr!Grr!Grr!Grr!
Grr!Grr!Grr!Grr!Grr!   Grr!
Grr!Grr!Grr!Grr!   Grr!   Grr!
Grr!   Grr!   Grr!   Grr!
Grr!   Grr!   Grr!
Grr!   Grr!
Grr!   Grr!
Grr!Grr!   Grr!Grr!

And the Moral of THIS Poem Is?

I had a little poem.
I wrote it in my head.
I went to bed –
forgot it all –
so wrote one more instead.

I wrote it on an envelope.
And when the thing was done
I hid it somewhere . . .
not sure where.
I'll write another one!

Shadow Talk

Psst!
It's me: your
shadow! I can
speak as well
you know –
thought
it's
time to
say HELLO. Tell you things
you   ought to know. Yes,   we're
close   but far apart. For   unlike
you   I have no heart: or soul,   or
eye,   or lung, or bone. Like   Sister
Moon,   I'm cold as stone, and   born
of   night and lack of light. That   Mother
Sun?   She's way too bright! So after   dusk
the   time is mine, to drink the dark   like
thick   black wine. But wait till late   to
tear   away, to jump the roof   -tops,
off to play. Midnight
mischief. Spooky stuff.
Haunting   houses.
Nothing   rough.
Night's   my day
I think   you'll find.
Night's   so right
for shadow   -kind.
You can't   escape
– I'm here   to stay.
I'm behind   you
all the   way!

HIDD_eN

Hidden in an acorn
a towering tree
hidden in a smile
a memory

Hidden in a crowd
a lonely soul
hidden in a ball
a winning goal

Hidden in a night
a day gone blind
hidden in a heart
a deed so kind

Hidden in a child
a youth grown old
hidden in a lie
a truth retold

Hidden in a cloud
a summer storm
hidden in an oak
a small acorn

Gorilla Gazing

(*London Zoo – Easter 2008*)

He sits and he stares
with them old brown eyes
beyond the glass
beyond my gaze
to a time
and a place
he's never known
yet somehow
seems to remember

Where the wind
shakes the trees
where the rain
wets the leaves
where there are
no walls at all

He sits and he stares
like an ancient sage
beyond the glass
beyond my gaze
to a world
long gone
and wonders why
we're all
so far
from home

Simply
St*rlight

Observe
the universe:
the expanse of space
and consider your place in it all . . .
and though you are small, like a
star, you are light, adrift in your life . . .
priceless and precious, brief
and unique – and this
is your time to
shine.

Clouds Like Us

(a poem for Mr Wordsworth)

```
@@@@
@@@
 ! !
! !
```

You're n e v e r lonely as a cloud
for like the sheep, you're with the crowd.
And then there's always loads to do
like soak a fete or barbecue.

Clouds are water – boiled you know.
We're recycled H20.
Stream to sea to cloud to rain
ever moving through a chain.

How we love it when it's warm.
For then we cook a mighty storm.
When it's time to help some flowers
we'll brew up those April showers.

Going back to our CV –
we've a range of skills you see
snow to hail to mist to fog
and forming shapes for you to spot!

Sunny spell? Oh we'll be back.
You'll need some rain – and that's a fact.
We're high as kites and cool as jazz.
That's clouds like us – our life's a gas!

!

!

!

!

Simply
St*rlight

Observe
the universe:
the expanse of space
and consider your place in it all . . .
and though you are small, like a
star, you are light, adrift in your life . . .
priceless and precious, brief
and unique – and this
is your time to
shine.

You, by Me

you are the light
that starts my day
that ups and burns
the night away

you are the drum
that beats my heart
that moves my limbs
for life to start

you are the sun
that brings the heat
that sweets the fruit
for me to eat

you are the clouds
that paint the sky
for me to drink
the rains you cry

you are the winds
that lift my wings
for me to fly
now here's the thing:

you
are the love
behind it all, no
you, no world
no life at
all

WhatDidYouDoAtSchoolToday?

Nothing.

Nothing?

Well, nothing much.

You did nothing much all day long?

Well . . . all right, Mum, if you really want to
   know,
I had 4 lessons
and 45 minutes of playtime
in which I went around with 3 friends.
For lunch I had 22 baked beans,
2 ½ fish fingers, a ¼ of a bread roll
and 1 banana.

I fed Nibbles, the class hamster,
2 sunflower seeds.
I wrote 1 poem.
I got 7/10 for a spelling test.
I did 16 fairly tricky maths questions.
And . . . I learned 5 very interesting things
about the ancient Egyptians, including
how they used to remove the brains
of their dead with a hook – MUM . . .
DO YOU EVER LISTEN TO A WORD I SAY?

Oh sorry, darling, what was that?

I said I removed my teacher's brain today!

What? Oh well done, you!
What would you like for tea?

Open **This** Door . . .

Inside you'll hear
sniggers and giggles
grumbles and groans
and a clock
that can never quite tick
slow enough.

Inside you'll find
biscuits and cakes
and a happy kettle
that boils
all day
every day
long.

Inside you'll meet
mums and sons
daughters and dads . . .
all day everyday people
all doing
extraordinary things.

Inside you'll be
in the engine room
in the calm within the storm
in the little greenhouse
where all the great
ideas grow.

Open this door
if you dare . . .

This is the
staffroom!

This Is Where...

... I learned to be.
And this is where I learned to read,
and write and count and act in plays,
and blossom in so many ways ...

And this is where I learned to sing,
express myself, and really think.
And this is where I learned to dream,
to wonder why and what things mean.

And this is where I learned to care,
to make good friends, to give, to share,
to kick, to catch, to race, to run.
This is where I had such fun.

And this is where I grew and grew.
And this is where? My primary school.

Life of *Flight*

Every night she would dream
of wings; watching, touching
even growing wings:
the clear, amber, veined wings
of dragonflies or bees;
the so-white wings of angels;
the taut, leathery wings of bats;
and, of course, the wings of birds –
doves, owls and starlings
and all those feathers, *feathers*;
more often, stranger wings
besides – from her own,
cavernous imagination, wings
stretching, tensing, readying
for her life of flight to come.

Scarecrow's Song

So   @@@@@
what are   @@@@
us scarecrows   ! !
scared of? Nothin' . . .   !
you can see. Oddly enough,   !
it's invisible
stuff that
scares
a
bod like
me. Let's begin with infinity –
through circlin' seasons four, just endless time to
stare and scare, forever bein' ignored. My other gripe?
That wicked sprite – the wind, as it whips my coat,
and beats my soul through wintry cold,
like a sail on a stormstruck
boat. But what of crows . . . ?
They're so-and-sos! They
laugh at me, they do!
Now don't say a
word, not a
dicky
bird – I
can't
scare a
flea – it's
true!

*Angel*ness

You
never
quite know
when you've
met
an
angel.
One may appear at any time at all. It won't have wings.
It won't wear white. Its angelness will
be invisible to the eye. Its human disguise
will be perfect in every way. And there'll be nothing
glamorous: just the quiet,
everyday business of
watching and
waiting
in case
you

fall.

If . . .

dinosaurs were real, then maybe
dragons were as well. And perhaps
one day they'll find a skeleton
beside a craggy cliff, far inside a cave:
a backbone and a tail, a jagged skull,
and those branch-like bones
where the wings would have been;
or even a whole dragon, perfectly
preserved in Siberian snow:
grey-green and scaly, those two top
canine fangs just jutting over the jaw,
the raging fire of the beast long lost
to the deep sleep of the dead,
those saggy eyelids closed
forever.

Spot *the* Fairy Tales...
(Five Little Senryus)

Little voice calling
an urgent word of warning
'The sky is falling!'

*

So no porky pies:
plenty of huffs and puffs . . . plus
a hot bot to boot!

*

'Hey, babe, way up there –
I've found neither lift nor stair –
please let down your hair!'

*

'My cunning planny –
if I can't nab that hoody,
I'll grab her granny!'

*

She's poshed up in bling.
Grooving with the future king.
Slipper fits. *Kerching!!!!!*

ANIMAL INSTINCTS

Wow, you really **WOLF** your food down, don't you?
  Do I?

Did you know you snuffle like a **boar**?
  I do?

Hey, you're looking a bit pale around the **gills**.
  Really?

Gosh, you look **dog** tired.
  What?

Perhaps you should take a **cat** nap.
  Eh?

And why are you getting all crabby?
  Now look here,
  you beastly thing
  don't you make
  a monkey out of me!
  I was having a whale of a time
  before you got all pig-headed
  stuck your beak in
  and started rabbiting on.
  Now please buzz off!

So, *Wolf* . . .

D'you know what you are? Me,
I'm not so sure. I know there's more
to you than I've been taught to see.

Beyond the silver coat and trophy tail.
Beneath the teeth that sink so well
into nice fresh flesh. Beyond the howl,

beneath the moon. Beyond the bedtime
tales that tell of how you moved to town:
of how you went tearing from door to door.

There must be more from time before
when you were free to be and do
without the mask of myths on you.

They . . .

. . . always talk about **the rain**.

They think they're always **right** when they're wrong.

They think that they know **everything** (about everything).

They say, 'Have you got a **brain** inside your head?'

They say, 'Yes, we're **nearly** there now.' Even if you're not.

They say, 'I'm not **grumpy**. I'm tired.' And, 'Life **isn't** fair.'

They say, 'Kids don't know what **bored** means these days.'

They say, 'Are you actually trying to **annoy** me?'

And, best of all, 'Which bit of **NO** don't you understand?'

No wonder they're called **GROAN-ups!**

The Cat

(for Alice, of course)

During the weekdays, the house
was quiet: empty of humans. The cat
had long tired of passing the time
with sleeping and moth-catching
and wall-staring and had recently taken to reading.
Luckily, the house was full of books.

There were books in every room. Best of all,
the cat enjoyed the books with poems.
Some poems, she observed, featured cats.
This pleased her greatly. Some of these cat poems,
she noticed, were good. Some very good.

Yet none, for her, expressed what it truly
feels like to be a cat. How it feels to be feline
and female. How it feels to be prodded
and poked by toddlers. How it feels
to be disrespected and distressed
by foxes and dogs. How it feels to be utterly terrified
by thunder and fireworks – and, worst of all,
how it feels to have to live nine long lives.

So the cat, over time, had taken to composing
her own verse; mainly short poems that she felt
spoke of her inner self: her true catness.

Her best poem (she believed) was the soul-searching
'Grey Moon in My Green Eyes', but she was also
secretly thrilled with the more upbeat kitty ditty
'Paws for Thought'. However, and maddeningly,
this all led to greater frustration. For, having
created her own poetry, she had no way
of writing the verses down. Reading,
as you may know, comes quite naturally to a cat.

But writing? With a paddy paw? Like a human
    drawing
with oven gloves on! The best she could achieve
was to spell out a few letters on the kitchen floor
with her Catkin Crunchies. But there were never
enough Catkin Crunchies! Even a full bowl would
    barely
spell the poem's title out! And all her efforts would
inevitably be scooped up by a hapless human and be
returned to her bowl.

RATS! she thought. Do all poets have to suffer like
    this?

Where Do You Get Your Ideas from?

From the **space** between my ears

from the *world* behind my eyes

from delving **deep inside** me

where *inspiration* lies

From memories that haunt me

from things I HEAR and see

from **mystical concoctions**

of **FACT** and *fantasy*

From **WORDS** that come and find me

from **dreaming** hard and long

from *life* and **books** and *music*

my poeMS: that's **where** they're from

Homes *sweet* Homes!

A hill is a home
for an ant
a cave is a home
for a bat
a mole has a hole
and so does a vole
a lap is a home
for a cat

A hive is a home
for a bee
a crab has its home
in the sea
and so does a seal
as well as an eel
a dog is a home
for a flea

For monkeys, a tree
for birdies, a nest
and itchy bugs reckon
a bedroom is best
from this can we learn
it's each to their own
whatever may be
their *home sweet home*!

Try *TIGER*...

COME,　　　　HUMAN.
Try　　　　　　tiger.
Grow twisting tail and amber
eyes, plenty whiskers, midnight
stripes. Let your nails curl out
as claws. Let your fists
morph into paws. Slink
slowly into jungle.
Blend awhile.
Be still.
Begin
to
plot　　　!!
your　　　!!
First kill ...　!!
You be wise.　!!
Now be wiser.　!!
Now be ... *tiger*!!

54

Shh!
or *Wilfred, the Boy Who Read . . .*

One day, at the age of three
Wilfred read the dictionary.
Every word from A to Zee
was stored inside his memory.

When he'd done, he went downstairs.
Still Wilfred's mum was unaware
the dictionary had now been read
by wordy Wilf – until he said

'Oh, Mother dear, I have a need.
For all I want to do is read.
Perchance I could try something hard
say. . . *Hamlet*, by the good old Bard?'

Wilf's request? As good as done.
The library later, Wilf and Mum
they asked for some of Shakespeare's plays.
The lady there was quite amazed:

'Oh dear boy! Please come and look
at stuff for you – perhaps a book
like *Naughty Nora's Naughty Day*?
or *Dolly Dolphin Swims Away*?

'Or *Cheeky Monkey's Full of Cheek*?
Sleepy Squirrel Goes to Sleep?
Or *Oh My Golly, Pirate Polly*?
Counting Kids with Charlotte Sheep?'

The library lady carried on
but bookworm boy by now had gone
and started one big literary feast
and soon he'd finished all of these:

Fluent French in Just a Week
British Sea Birds: Beak by Beak
How to Grow the Perfect Rose
The Fall of Rome (in Latin Prose).

Mum said later, in a huff:
'It's time for tea. I've had enough!'
But Wilfred, no, he wouldn't budge
he'd rather have a book to munch.

'Shh!' said Wilf, then, 'Mummy, dear –
I need to read. Is that not clear?
I've lots to learn. I'm only three.
The library is the place for me!'

And then he read through *British Kings*
and *How to Play the Violin*
and Shakespeare's plays (plus all his sonnets)
and *How to Build a Real Rocket*.

In your library should you see
a bookish boy, about aged three –
Shh! That's Wilf (though maybe not).
But keep it down. He reads. A LOT.

PUZZL!NG

DON'T

do

a

space

jigsaw

out

in

those

bits

place

float

all over

will

the

Random Ralph

A random boy was Random Ralph,
for random words popped out his mouth –
like PIFFLESNOG and TWIP and PISH
and SNOTTLEPOTS and FARPLEFISH.
Such randomness popped out his mouth.
A random boy was Random Ralph!

What Can You Do with a Football?

Well . . .

You can
kick it – you can catch
it – **you can bounce it** – all
around. YOU CAN GRAB IT *you can*
pat it *you can roll it* – on the ground.
You can throw it you can head it
you can hit it – **with a bat**. You can
biff it you can boot it YOU CAN SPIN
IT you can SHoot it You can
drop it *you can stop it. Just
like that!*

An
Ode
to
Keith,
My
Old
Guitar

Listen up
my six-string
chum ... for
you're the
rea-
son
that
I
strum,
and
pick
and
plunk
and
have
the
FUNK.
Keith: you
are my #1.
You're brown. You're
wood. You're round. That's ...
good. You're thin. You're wide.
You've ... dust inside. You're
where I go when I feel low.
You help me lose
the BLUES you know. You
ROCK ... you ROLL. You're FOLK
with SOUL. And yes, you SWING,
you crazy thing. You jingle,
jangle. And you twang.
You're my guitar.
I'm so YOUR
FAN.

KILLER KENNING

I
dive
down deep
I dwell in the dark
oh yes, indeedy I'm a . . .

jaw-breaker
ship-shaker
movie-maker
breath-taker
super-sniffer
flesh-ripper
toothy-terror
finny-fella
mad-marauder
fish-in-water
crazy-creature
lurve-to-eat-ya!

SH...SH...SH...

SHARK!!!

Ode $_2$ H$_2$O

You know the greatest tragedy?
that you and me can never be
our moods are just too contrary

I love you, H$_2$O

You make the clouds that charm the sky
whilst I make smoke that clouds the eye
for you're the stuff of life, not I

I love you, H$_2$O

If I could form the tears you make
or oceans, clouds or rivers, lakes
the sky would cry, the earth would shake

I love you, H$_2$O

I'll always want you from afar
and envy yes, and so admire
but did you know my name is . . . fire?

I love you, H$_2$O

The *Carrot*

and the

Hat

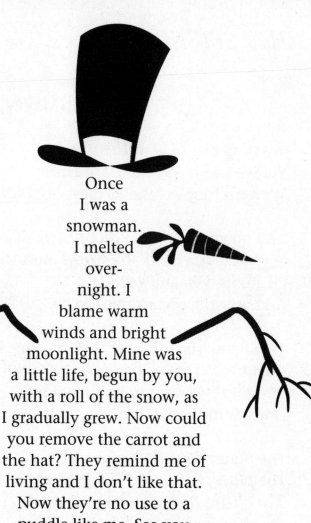

Once
I was a
snowman.
I melted
over-
night. I
blame warm
winds and bright
moonlight. Mine was
a little life, begun by you,
with a roll of the snow, as
I gradually grew. Now could
you remove the carrot and
the hat? They remind me of
living and I don't like that.
Now they're no use to a
puddle like me. See you
next year . . . *hopefully.*

Hey, SCIENCE!
STOP.
An Answer, Please

We need one of your *theories*.
You've told us how it *all* began.
With nothing . . . then a great *big bang*!

And how the *sun* and *moon* were made
and what you think the *world* must weigh.
Of atoms, yes, and *gravity*.
And how the oceans came to be.

Then land, then life, then wheel, then car
then trips to Mars and *blah blah blah*.
But *what* we want to know and how –
is why's the world so really . . . *WOW*?

The honey bee? The polar bear?
The *platypus?* Or don't you care?
This little rock on which we dwell:
the chance of *life*? Well who can tell?

So take your time to ponder it.
And look around the world a bit.
Or peep into your *microscope*.
Your answer will be good. *We hope!*

What's in My *Mind?*

Scientists (apparently)
are baffled by the mind.
To them, the brain's a mystery.
But me? I'm sure I'd find . . .

The Wells of Creativity.
The Lake of Deep Regret.
The Fields of Marvellous Memories.
The Forest of I-Forget.

The Caves of All Times Tables.
The Creek of Awful Jokes.
The Woods of Dreams and Nightmares.
The Vale of Favourite Quotes.

Now if I looked much further
I'm sure I'd reach a place
and that would be Head Office –
right here, behind my face.

Inside? Well, rows of buttons
commands of every kind:
like 'EAT' and 'BLINK' and 'SMILE' and 'YAWN' –
I think that's what I'd find.

An Ode to My *Brain*

You're a schemer.
You're a dreamer.
You're the bit
that makes me me.

You're all spongy.
You're all gungy.
And you help me
feel and see.

You sit inside
my head up here.
You drive me around.
You help me hear.

You're creative.
You're inventive.
You're the bit
that makes me tick.

You're a tiny
little library.
You're the thing
that makes me think.

For a grown-up
or a baby
you're amazing . . . ly
BRAINY!

September
Seagulls

At last!
the seagulls sigh
as the last car
leaves the car park.
At last!
the seagulls sigh
at the thought
of no more toddlers
playing chase-the-birdie
no more radios
playing 'Mr Blue Sky'
and no more showy-offy sea-surfers
playing yo!-there-ladies.

At last!
the seagulls sigh
but then remember
the cold, the wind
the endless rain
and worst of all
the no more
curry-flavoured pasties
the no more
tuna-mayo sarnies
the no more
semi-soggy 99 ice creams.
Drat!
the seagulls sigh.

Go, *Poem . . .*

There, little poem.
You're finished at last.
From weeks of tweaking
you've finally passed.

You're ready for roaming,
to find your own page,
and maybe a voice
to give you a stage.

You're out of my system,
my pen and my brain.
Let's hope you'll be read
again and again.

And so, as your author,
it's me, signing off.
The pleasure's been mine.
Go poem, find love . . .

Journey to the Centre of

JAMES

in six actual facts

1. As a boy, James was BONKERS about books (especially Tintins) – and still is. He was also GAGA about guitars (especially electrics) – and still is. Saturday mornings would begin with him strumming along on his tennis racket to his favourite radio show. Later on he'd cycle down to the shop to buy two comics and then whizz back to read them on his bed. Nice!

2. James has been playing guitar – REAL ONES, NOT JUST TENNIS RACKETS – for over thirty-five years now. But he played biscuit-tin drums in his first and short-lived band The Electric Spiders. Sadly, the band broke up one morning when his best friend's mum wanted her drumsticks – well, knives and forks – back. Five years later, James's first school band, Villain, was booed off at its first concert during the first song! Not nice!

3. James wrote his first poem when he was seventeen. All he remembers was that it was entitled 'One'. He wrote it for the school magazine, but they didn't like it and didn't include it! James didn't give up though, for ONLY twenty years later he had his first poem 'Rules for School Trips' published. Very nice!

4. James loves school-dinner custard – as long as it's yellow and not pink. Pink custard? Yuck!

5. James used to be a trainspotter. But he's given it up. HONESTLY! No, really. Seriously. Nowadays he travels by train to schools all over the UK and abroad and does most of his writing on trains. This makes the drivers VERY cross. Ouch!

6. It takes him at least three months to write each poem. Some take years. Fussy or what? Actually, this book took five years to write, and he scrapped over a thousand poems to find the ones he wanted to include here. James writes poems because a) it gives him something to do with all his daydreaminess and b) he loves words, and always has, and he believes that poems are the best fun you can have with words. His favourite word? *Rhythm*. Funky!